Life Choices

SOME RELATIONS ARE DIFFERENT

(Alias 'thoughtful girl')

NEHA JAIN

INDIA · SINGAPORE · MALAYSIA

Notion Press

Old No. 38, New No. 6
McNichols Road, Chetpet
Chennai - 600 031

First Published by Notion Press 2019
Copyright © Neha Jain 2019
All Rights Reserved.

ISBN 978-1-68466-818-2

LOVE is an eternal feeling. It just drives your life crazy... yet mesmerises you. Everyone has his/her memories of love... some good, some bad and some mixed. This is a simple love story—the love story of Vivan and Anubhuti. They were a simple lad and lass, like any other boy or girl. But what made them different was the inseparable love between them which we will discover gradually.

Contents

Acknowledgments　7

Prologue　9

Part-1

Graduation Course in College:
Where They Both First Met Each Other　13

Part-2

Post Graduation Time: Where
They—for Once—Completely Lost Each Other　37

Part-3

Earning Time: Where They Actualise
Their Relationship　43

Part-4

Decision Time: When Real Decision
Changes Their Lives Forever　61

Part-5

New Beginning: A New Era of Relationship Starts　67

Acknowledgments

This is my first novel that I have written and published. I am highly thankful to God to have given me the strength and creativity to pen down such a story with his pious blessings. Then, obviously my parents without whose upbringing and unconditional care, it would have been seriously impossible to achieve anything. I thank my siblings and husband who always listened to me patiently each time and gave their valuable feedback. Last, but not the least my close friends who always motivated me when I lost track. I am very thankful to everyone who was part of my writing journey.

◈ ◈ ◈

Prologue

This book is for every other opposite gender friends who start loving each other and have to leave their love due to unconventional society norms. They have a beautiful relationship like Vivan and Anubhuti starting from best friends to being sweethearts. I don't think it's wrong to love a person because true love happens naturally. Do we have to figure out all feasibilities before?. That's really absurd. Sorry for being rude. But it's the reality that we need have to be bounded by certain conditions to love otherwise just compromise and move on. It's not easy guys. Rare lovers get united heavenly forever. We have to choose between family and love.

Vivan and Anubhuti too had to choose love or friendship. It is their story with different phases of their relationship. Will they be united forever? Will love conquer family? Do they have life choices coherent to their love or compromise? Whatever they have to decide changes everything for better or else? Let's start reading and get to know their love journey.

◆ ◆ ◆

PART-1

"So bonded and deep was their friendship that they understand each other even in silence."

– By thoughtful girl

Graduation Course in College: Where They Both First Met Each Other

The day was progressing as usual for Anubhuti when she was on her way to college. She was an intelligent student with simple looks. Her ambition was to be successful and independent in her life. She always started at 8.30 am in the morning to reach her college at 9. This was the time when her first lecture, which was Chemistry began. It is but obvious that she was pursuing B.Sc. (Gen) from DU and she lived in Kamla Nagar in Delhi. The college and her home were at a distance of just a few kilometres which was manageable in one hour to and fro.

Her father was a middle-income businessman having a kids' garment shop in Kamla Nagar itself. Her mom was a spectacular homemaker. As she was the only child in the family, she loved being pampered all the time.

As always she reached her college on time. Her college was one of the topmost of the Delhi University's North campus colleges—"Hindu College". It was one of the oldest and most famous ones. The college had a huge building with lots of lecture halls, an administrative area and a canteen with lush surroundings. As usual, her best friend Vivan was waiting for her at the college gate. He was a handsome guy with a notoriously mischievous nature. He lived in Shahdara with his parents and a brother. His father had a business dealing in automobile parts, and his mother was a teacher in a primary school. His brother was in Class 10. He waved a "hi" to her, to which she smiling responded.

Vivan was the first student she met on her very first day in college. Both of them were looking for their classrooms. At the noticeboard, both were searching for their names along with the respective lecture-room number. There was massive chaos as all the students were in a hurry to be in time for their first lecture. Suddenly Vivan felt as if someone had patted him on the back. He looked back and saw a worried girl staring at him.

He said, "Yes, may I help you?"

The girl replied, "I am sorry if I am troubling you."

He said smilingly, "Not at all...Tell me what I can do for you."

She said in a hurried tone, "Please, can you help me in finding my lecture-room?"

He promptly replied, "Ok... What's your good name?"

She replied in a second, "Anubhuti."

He turned to the noticeboard instantly and started searching for her name. After a few seconds, he remarked, "Hey, we both are in the same batch... LR -2(GF)."

Before he could turn back, he could hear the same girly voice asking him to come quickly to the lecture-room.

He ran after her. Both of them found seats for each other and settled down. All the students stood up to welcome their first lecturer. After all of them were in their seats again, the lecture began.

A middle-aged gentleman with a raw voice introduced himself, "I am Mr. Nalin Mehta. I will be teaching you Chemistry." All eyes were glued to his face as he said this. He continued further, "Today is your first day in this college. So I won't bore you with chemical equations... let's get to know each other today."

Everybody started laughing, looking at each other and the lecturer. He had changed a serious environment into a happy one, comforting the tension-ridden faces. All the students introduced themselves. Suddenly, the bell rang and the lecture ended. Fortunately, that being the first day, there was only one lecture in the timetable. All the students started exiting the class with sighs of relief.

Anubhuti patted Vivan on the back again, and he laughingly turned to her and said, "You always do this to call a person."

She laughed along with him replying, "No, I have different ways to call different persons and this is for you."

They both giggled again. After walking some distance from the classroom to the college gate, Anubhuti said, "I forgot to ask your name."

Vivan stood silent for a while and looked at Anubhuti who was giving him a curious look. She said, "What happened? It's ok if you don't want to tell."

Vivan suddenly started laughing and said, "Nothing yaar, I thought if you also had helped me find my LR room on nb."

Anubhuti started hitting him on his back and he said, "Sorry yaar, I was kidding… My name is Vivan."

Anubhuti stopped hitting him and said, "Chalo maaf kiya…tum bhi kya yaad karoge."

This was the start of their friendship which grew day-by-day.

Everyday Vivan waited at the college gate for Anubhuti to accompany her to the lecture-room. Both loved each other's company so much that if any day either of them needed to take leave, the other one obliged as well. They were famous in their batch and among their lecturers for their special friendship. Everyone knew that they came together, sat together and left together.

They were both now heading towards their lecture-room according to the timetable. Both Vivan and Anubhuti were very studious and never missed their lectures unless there was an emergency. This fact was well known among their batch mates as they were the only ones who were always present in the backup classes if there were any missed ones. That day too there was a backup class after lunch as Mr. Sharma who taught them Mathematics was on leave. They both settled next to each other and their other batch mates also joined in. The physics lecture had started and their lecturer Mr. Robin D'Souza started with "Newton's Law of Gravity." He was a serious man with a strict nature as suggested by his behaviour towards his students. Anyways, the lecture ended as the bell rang, and all the students smiled silently at each other.

The next to come in was Mrs. Krutika, the English lecturer. She was very amiable and fun-loving, to the extent that she never scolded her students in any event. All the students welcomed her with sweet smiles. She signalled them to sit and announced that she would be starting the epic love story "Romeo and Juliet". The class started on a romantic note. Mrs. Krutika asked everybody to express their feelings about love.

Every student shared his/her own story except Vivan and Anubhuti. According to them, they had never fallen in love, so they couldn't express it. The whole class started laughing and smiled at each other.

The bell rang and everybody rushed to the canteen. Their college had a wide variety of dishes served in the cafeteria, which were lip-smacking and yet very affordable for the students. The cafeteria was a wide-spread space with a huge sitting area. The furniture in the canteen looked elegant as compared to other DU colleges.

The canteen was crowded with everyone rushing to collect their orders from the service counter. There was a long queue at the cashier's desk and the ordering table. Vivan and Anubhuti had their own favourite spot in the canteen area in a corner space near the TV setup. They were both addicted to TV. While everyone was busy munching their favourite cuisine, they both enjoyed the TV telecast of "Pyar ka dard hai meetha-meetha pyaara pyaara." It was their favourite programme. How paradoxical! Even though the two of them claimed to have never experienced the feeling of love, they had their own well-enjoyed half an hour lunch break, and everybody in the college knew this.

After the lunch break, the turmoil of lecture sessions again started, which generally ended between 4 and 5 in the evening. But their college day never ended at that time. After college, they always went for a coffee at CCD at Kamla Nagar. At that time, they both discussed college issues and of course personal problems as well. They were actually such good friends that they never hid anything from each other and there was an unusual trust between them.

After an hour or so, they both headed towards their respective houses and at that moment they ended their contact until next morning in the college. They never talked to each other during the time they were at home, through any means, even if there was an emergency. This was an unsaid rule between them. So bonded and deep was their friendship that they understand each other even in silence.

That day was another usual college day for both of them as she accompanied Vivan from the college gate to their lecture-room. That day they had only one lecture, so they became free very early. After the lecture got over, they decided to ditch CCD and planned to see the movie of their favourite star "Shahrukh".

They went to Connaught Place through metro, and then headed towards Regal movie hall and purchased two tickets for both of them. There was a huge crowd at the movie hall. They also purchased a bucket full of popcorn and two cold drinks. As usual both paid for their share of the purchases, which was a strict rule made by Anubhuti. They entered the movie theatre. The movie was about to start as commercials had started playing on the screen. They had got balcony seats as desired by Vivan. The seats in the theatre hall were very comfortable. The ambience was made even cosier with the air conditioner on. The two young people settled into their seats comfortably. The movie commenced in a while.

Both of them started enjoying it along with the lip-smacking popcorn and chilled soft drinks. Then came the interval. Vivan asked Anubhuti if she was enjoying the movie or not. She replied softly, "Yes." Then the interval ended and the romantic drama continued. They were watching the climax where the hero fights for the heroine and gets her. The heroine was running towards the train which the hero had got into. Yes, you are guessing it right. It was Dilwale Dulhania Le Jayenge (DDLJ).

Anubhuti suddenly became emotional watching the melodramatic scene of the movie and grasped Vivan's hand tightly. Vivan became self-conscious at this sudden action of hers. He just watched her with amazement in silence. Anubhuti came out of her dilemma and observed him. She felt shy suddenly and left his hand quickly. He just laughed at her. She became even more shy.

The movie ended and both stood up from their seats and headed towards the exit door of the hall. They were silent until they reached McDonald's at CP. Vivan asked Anubhuti, "What would you like to have?"

She replied after a few seconds, "Mc Aloo Tikki burger."

Vivan placed the order at the counter as "Two Mc Aloo Tikki burgers and two cold drinks."

Again obviously the bill was divided into two exact halves as per their rule. The counter boy gave the receipt to him and told him to wait for the order to arrive. Both were silent again and in their own thought processes. Suddenly the order arrived. Vivan took the tray and they looked around for two seats. Anubhuti signalled him towards an empty corner seat. They seated themselves comfortably and he asked her to start eating. She said, "Hmm... you also eat."

Vivan started a conversation with her about college and studies to avoid the silence between them. She too got involved in talking. Both of them had finished their portions. They watched each other for a second and smiled at each other. They then left McDonald's and headed towards the Rajiv Chowk metro station. They then purchased the tickets from the ticket counter and waited for the train to arrive at the platform. They climbed onto the train as it arrived. Anubhuti didn't sit separately in the women's coach. Both of them stood near the door of the compartment as no seats were available. It was highly crowded inside the train.

Suddenly Vivan asked Anubhuti whether she had enjoyed the day or not. She signalled in the affirmative with a movement of her head. Vivan gave a cute smile in response to her. She too smiled. The train was about to reach the station where she had to alight. Vivan suddenly said, "I like you Anubhuti." She listened dumbstruck.

The station arrived and she just got down from the train. She turned back and saw Vivan waving a goodbye towards her. She too bid goodbye to him. Both were thinking about each other long after reaching home and the day ended with normal chores.

The college days were passing as usual for both of them. Then came the exams and both fared well in them. Their graduation course was progressing year by year.

They were becoming too close day-by-day but never shared their feelings for each other.

The months passed, and it was their last day in college. There was a farewell get-together for all the students. Anubhuti wore a purple suit paired with silver dangles. She looked gorgeous. Vivan too looked dashing in a cream kurta-pyjama with a red bandhej dupatta. As usual Vivan was waiting for her at the college gate. Both of them looked towards each other in astonishment. Then with a smile they proceed towards the college auditorium. Vivan complimented her and she too reciprocated smilingly. They found two seats near stage. Performances started in a rocking manner. Everyone was enjoying it. Then came the casual call for dances in the end. Vivan asked Anubhuti for a dance by offering his hand. She accepted the proposal. Both were very much wrapped up in each other. Vivan slowly came close to her and whispered in her ear, "I really like you a lot." She became shy and went outside the auditorium. He ran towards her and touched her hand. She was controlling her deep breaths. Anubhuti turned to him and said, "I too like you a lot."

Vivan gave her a broad smile and said, "Really?"

She shyly signalled "Yes" with her head. He tightened his grip on her hand. Anubhuti said, "Let's have some snacks. I am very hungry," to avoid his constant attention. Vivan replied, "Sure. Let's go."

Vivan picked up a plate near the food stalls and grasped her hand saying, "We both will have from one plate. I hope you don't mind." She gave him a smirking look. Both were enjoying each other's attention. He put a spring roll into her mouth. She too put a samosa into his mouth. Both started smiling at each other in affection. Anubhuti looked her watch. It was 5:30 p.m. She was getting late for home as she had promised her dad that she would reach home by 6 p.m. and it would take her almost half an hour to reach home from college. Vivan noticed her tense look. He consoled her saying, "I will drop you home today as dad has gifted me a new bike today." She was relieved and happily went back with him. He dropped her near to her home as others could misunderstand their relationship as her family was very conservative in such things.

She was about to leave him but before she could leave, Vivan looked into her eyes and said, "Please keep in touch always. We will meet soon on our convocation day."

Anubhuti was silent as she knew that the convocation was a month later, and she did not know how she would manage without seeing him.

She smiled suddenly and said, "Yes, for sure. Take care. Bye."

He too bid goodbye. She left. Vivan watched her going till she reached the end of the road from where she took a turn towards her home. He left only after that. They were both thinking about each other every single moment till then.

Because of their unsaid rule of no contact after college, numbers were never exchanged between them.

The days were passing miserably for both of them as they both wanted desperately to see each other as soon as possible. Then came the fortunate day. Since morning both were quite excited to meet each other, whereas their family members were assuming their happiness as due to the completion of their graduation.

Anubhuti reached college and saw Vivan waiting for her. She waved at him to which he reciprocated smilingly and both were silent on their way to the auditorium. They occupied two empty seats adjacent to each other in the third row. All the students were gathering and soon the auditorium was fully crowded.

Then came the voice of their Dean from the stage. He congratulated all the students on the successful completion of their graduation and wished them well in their future prospects. Then the Vice-chancellor came on stage by invitation of the Dean. He gave a short applauding speech to the students guiding them on their vibrant future. He then started distributing degrees to all the students according to their stream and roll number. Both Anubhuti and Vivan went onto the stage in response to their respective calls. They both congratulated each other wholeheartedly.

Now the Dean invited all to the lunch organised by the college. Everybody proceeded towards the lunch area in the lawn in front of the auditorium. Vivan took a plate and grasped Anubhuti's hovering hand guiding her towards the plates. She smiled and they both started taking a stroll around the dishes. She said to Vivan, "Today I will eat the food of your choice."

He happily served all of his favourite dishes on the plate. They found an empty table and seated themselves comfortably. Vivan gave her a morsel of food in her mouth. She also did the same and both continued till they were full. Vivan stood up and said to her, "Now dessert of your choice."

She followed him in amusement and took two pieces of gulab jamun for both of them. They again fed each other affectionately.

Anubhuti looked towards Vivan charmingly. Vivan noticed it and she shyly avoids his eye-contact. Vivan took her hand in his hand and looked into her eyes. She was shy again. He said, "I love you Anubhuti... I really love you a lot... main kabhi tumse keh nahi paya but iss ek mahine ne mujhe yeh ehsaas karaya ki main tumhare bina ek pal bhi nahi reh sakta... you are my life."

Anubhuti listened intensely looking into his eyes. She was silent. Vivan asked her whether he meant something to her or not. She wanted to speak, but something was preventing her. Vivan comforted her shoulders and noticed her silent reaction.

He said, "I know you love me and something is holding you back. I want to know what that is."

She looked at him earnestly and said, "My ethical values will not allow me to do so."

Vivan knew this but wanted to hear it from her. He consoled her saying, "I know, but we can give a try if you agree."

She was lost in deep thoughts evaluating every prospect. She realised that Vivan was waiting for her answer. She just said, "Goodbye" and left. Vivan watched awkwardly letting her go, but finally ran after her and stood in front of her. She was taken aback by his sudden action. He asked her, "I want your reply... Yes or No."

She replied, "Let's meet tomorrow at 4 p.m. at CCD," and left.

Both had various complex thoughts until the next day began.

The day was passing at a much faster pace than normal for both of them. The actual time came finally as both met at the decided place and time. Vivan looked at Anubhuti affectionately as they took a table for two.

He asked her, "What would you like to have?"

She replied after a little thought, "I would have cold coffee."

He asked, "Nothing to eat?"

She promptly said, "No."

He then ordered two cold coffees. Anubhuti was looking away from him as if avoiding him. He initiated the conversation asking about her plans for the future. She replied that she was not sure right then, and again got engaged in her thoughts.

He looked for a while at her in silence until they were interrupted by the waiter with their order. The waiter put two large cups of coffee in front of them and left. Vivan took his cup and asked her to do the same. She reluctantly took it. He said to her, "You look disturbed."

She looked at him and replied smilingly, "It is not so."

He looked deeply into her eyes and said, "I know it is and why it is."

She was taken aback by his statement. They both knew in their hearts but didn't want to make each other tense. So profound was their love.

Vivan took her hand in his palm and said, "I don't want to make you stressed. I like you smiling."

She became emotional and said, "I know that dear."

He said, "Let's make a deal."

She asked in curiosity, "What?"

He said, "Let's leave all things to destiny."

She smiled. He smiled too seeing her relax a bit. They then continued discussing their future plans. Both of them decided to do an MBA. It was a huge decision for both of them which also would help to realise their personal destiny.

Anubhuti said to Vivan, "I have to leave now as I am getting late."

He dropped her at the same place near her house. Both bid goodbye to each other. But this time a rule got changed between them. They decided to contact each other through Gmail. They exchanged their id's for the very first time since college and finally took leave of each other.

Days passed by as usual for both of them. Their only means of contact was e-mail and text chatting because video chatting was banned between them. Again an unsaid rule which was maintained with dignity by both of them. They usually discussed about CAT, MAT and all MBA coaching stuff. They now had decided to study together to prepare for various MBA entrance exams. The venue decided was CCD again which was near to Anubhuti's house as decided by Vivan for her convenience.

The two of them went there daily at 12 noon to prepare for their MBA exams. Finally the exam dates were fast approaching, so they had decided to revise by themselves at home till the exams. Anubhuti was waiting for Vivan at the examination centre. She was looking quite nervous. Vivan was watching her while he came up to her. He touched her shoulder from behind. She got startled in shock and he started laughing. She hit him saying, "You are very mean. Itna intezaar kyun karaya mujhe?"

He stopped laughing and taking her hand, replied, "Sorry for the delay yaar and I am mean only for you."

She looked at him awkwardly. He couldn't control his laughter again.

They both went inside the examination hall. It was their CAT exam. They stood comfortably after finding their seats according to the seating arrangement on the blackboard. Both signalled "best of luck" to each other. The exam started and everyone in the class was handling the tough questionnaire in those most difficult three hours. As the exam ended, both met at the centre's gate.

Vivan asked her, "How was the exam?"

She didn't answers. He asked her, "Are you fine?"

She replied, "Yes... exam was fine... how was yours?"

He said, "Fine."

They went towards the metro station and took the metro towards Shahdara. Both were still silent. Vivan could figure out from her stressed face that there was something wrong with her. He asked, whispering in her ears, "Is there a problem, yaar? You can share with me; see if I can help you out."

She looked towards his face and replied with a mysterious face, "No."

He again pressurised her, "Then what is it?"

She gave a strained reply, "Nothing."

Her station soon arrived and she left with a goodbye to him. But Vivan knew there was something. He too went home thinking about her. The two of them were thinking about each other the whole night.

In this manner they gave many MBA entrance exams but with silence between them. They didn't talk through Gmail either during this period. Now finally comes a day when the CAT results were about to be announced. Both were anxious and wanted to talk to each other. Vivan emailed her "Hey... can we meet?"

She replied after much thought, "Yes... same place... same time."

Vivan reached there before time and waited for her. Anubhuti found him waiting there when she arrived. Both looked towards each other and wished "hi". She sat down in front of the table where Vivan was already seated. He asks her very politely "Are you nervous? I am very nervous."

She said, "Yes, I am."

The results were expected at 1pm. Vivan had brought his lappy with him and took it out from the bag. He then logged into it and opened the CAT result website. There appeared a box to write the roll number to check the result of a candidate on the website. Anubhuti said, "You first." Vivan entered his roll number and his result was about to load. He crossed his fingers in fear and started murmuring his prayers with closed eyes. He was a Muslim. She looked at him affectionately. His result downloaded on the website. Anubhuti shouted with joy "Hurray....you have cleared it." He opened his eyes joyfully. Vivan then entered Anubhuti's roll number and her result was about to load on the website. She caught his hand tightly in tension and he prayed again for her. After a while, Vivan felt her leave the grip on his hand. He opened his eyes slowly and saw on her result page "Not cleared." He was shocked and saw Anubhuti with tears in her eyes. He immediately consoled her saying, "Don't worry... there will be other good opportunities for you."

She replied in haste, "But why not this one for me?"

He took her hand and said, "Because God has something better than this for you."

She looked at him and cried again. He consoled her all the way dropping her near her home.

She left him without saying goodbye for the first time. He watched her leave until she vanished at the corner. He was feeling very bad for her but nothing was in his hands. He reached his home lost in sad thoughts. He spent the whole night thinking about her. Several days passed like this with no communication between them. Vivan thought she needed some space so didn't disturb her.

A few days passed in this manner with no communication between them, but Vivan was really keen to talk to her as was Anubhuti. Finally, he received a mail from her on Gmail. He was very happy to see the message which said, "Hey Vivan... how r u? Today our MAT result will be out at 12 noon. Please meet me." Vivan was awaiting her mail that day but was not very sure about it. He got ready and reached the same meeting place as always at 11.45 a.m. and waited for her. At 11.55 a.m. Anubhuti arrived and found him waiting for her. Vivan raised a "hi" to her to which she responded. She sat opposite to him at the table where Vivan was already seated. Vivan asked her how she was. She replies promptly, "I am fine Vivan. How are you?"

He said, "I am fine. I was just worried about you." Anubhuti looked at him earnestly and said, "I am fine, Vivan. Don't worry. Let's check our results."

Vivan opened his laptop and logged into the MAT website. Both were quite tense. Vivan entered his roll number and the result was about to load for him on the site. He closed his eyes as usual and prayed. Anubhuti shouted in joy for him, "Hey Vivan... you have cleared." He opened his eyes and saw his result. He said, "Thanks Anubhuti."

Now he entered Anubhuti's roll number. He again closed his eyes and prayed for her. Anubhuti as always had caught his hand tightly in hers in tension. Vivan opened his eyes after a while. He saw her result and turned towards Anubhuti who was crying in joy. He hugged her tightly and said aloud, "I knew you would clear it."

Both of them sat in the same position for a while until Anubhuti realised the surroundings and drew herself back. He wiped her tears and she still had her hand in his. Vivan asked her enchantingly, "Where is my party?"

She said, "Now."

He replied, "Not here. We will plan it."

She said, "As you say."

Both wanted to leave as both wished to celebrate it with their family members. Anubhuti said suddenly, "Today I will go on my own."

He said, "Ok madam. As you wish."

Both bid goodbye to each other and left.

The two of them shared their happiness with their family on reaching home and the day ended on a joyous note. Days were passing happily and both communicated with each other through Gmail discussing which college to take admission for MBA. They both went for the admission process and got selected to their respective colleges. Both then decided to have a party. The place decided was The Taj hotel for a lavish lunch. Vivan as usual reached before time and Anubhuti found him waiting for her. She looked gorgeous in a white suit. He too looked quite handsome in a black trouser and a white linen shirt. Both looked their best that day. Both smiled at each other. He then offered her a seat and sat beside her. The waiter came up and asked for their order. Vivan signalled Anubhuti, to which she responded by ordering Vivan's favourite. He then ordered her favourite dishes. The waiter left. Vivan appreciated Anubhuti saying, "You are looking like an angel today."

She smilingly replied, "You too are a handsome dude today."

Both laughed. Meanwhile the waiter arrived with their order. Vivan served Anubhuti and she reciprocated the gesture.

Anubhuti said, "I want to feed you the first bite with my hands."

He retorted, "Why not madam ?"

Both then enjoyed the lunch. They then ordered the dessert. In the meantime, Vivan looked at Anubhuti with a sad smile and said, "I know today is our happiest day, but the saddest also."

She looked towards Vivan intently and said "I know dear. We will be apart in terms of distance, but not in our hearts."

He held her hand lovingly until they were disturbed by the waiter with their desserts. Both ate it in silence and as per their rule the bill was divided among them equally. Both decided to communicate through Gmail as before regularly and bid goodbye to each other with sad smiles.

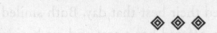

PART-2

"Patience and time sometimes gives us that thing which remains in our heart that we could never express."

– By thoughtful girl

Post Graduation Time: Where They—for Once—Completely Lost Each Other

———— ❧ ————

After settling into their respective MBA colleges, they contacted each other daily through Gmail for a few days. But later on, they both got busy in their hectic schedules. They couldn't even get time to miss each other. Things were going on at hectic pace in their courses. Lectures, seminars and presentations made both of them busy. They could not realise that there is some personal aspect of life also. Their families were in touch with them, but even they couldn't contact them daily due to their busy schedules. But because they knew it was only temporary, they were not worried. Both Vivan and Anubhuti had so-called new friends in their college now, but they could never fill each other's place in their lives. They were just formal acquaintances.

Time swept by until their final year when placements started. They both got placed in good MNC organisations. Their families were very happy with knowing this. Now was the time they thought of contacting each other once again. Vivan mailed Anubhuti about his placement. He got a reply from Anubhuti about her placement. Both shared their joyous moments with each other. But there was a problem. This time also they had to be separated. Both had got jobs in different cities. So they consoled each other by deciding that soon they would be sharing their contact numbers after reaching their respective job locations. This gave them some relief.

But they didn't know that God had already decided their fate after that day. It was a new chapter of their life after which everything was going to change for both of them. Not only their present life but also the future one. It was a new landmark in their lives. As it is always said, God always listens to our prayers. It was the time for their prayers to be answered. Their dreams were going to be fulfilled, which they never thought could be. Patience and time sometimes give us that thing which remains in our hearts but we could never express.

Anubhuti and Vivan's story was about to take a huge U-turn. A turn which would be deciding their fate. Both reach home after their convocations. Preparations then started for their departure. Moms packed everything and instructed them over every little thing. Dads gave them advice on how to cope in a new city. Siblings were happy as new gifts awaited them.

Finally they both went to their respective job locations, that is, Vivan to Bangalore and Anubhuti to

Hyderabad. It took some time for both of them to settle down. So they didn't contact each other during that time. Ultimately both remembered their promise and this time Anubhuti contacted him one fine day.

PART-3

"A love is more prime to two lovers, it was their
friendship for them."

– By thoughtful girl

Earning Time: Where They Actualise Their Relationship

—⟋—

Vivan got a call from Anubhuti one fine day. It was an unknown number. He picked up the call and there was a familiar voice on the other side, "Hey Vivan... This is Anubhuti here."

Vivan becomes so happy on listening to her voice after so many days that he couldn't utter a single word for a few seconds. Anubhuti said again, "What happened Vivan... Are you ok?"

He gathered his wits and replied, "Hey Anubhuti... how are you...I am fine."

She smilingly said, "I am good. I got your number from our college friend Shruti."

They asked each other about their job whereabouts. As they were at their respective work locations, they couldn't talk much and decided to talk through Gmail at night.

Both were quite excited to talk to each other after a long time. Vivan reached home after work and opened his personal laptop. He opened his Gmail eagerly. He saw a ping from Anubhuti to which he replied quickly. Both talked about general topics for a few minutes. Then suddenly Vivan said to Anubhuti, "I miss you, yaar."

She became happy to hear this but just replied, "Hmm."

She then ended the conversation abruptly saying, "I think we should sleep now. It's too late and we both have office tomorrow."

Both bid goodbye but thoughts were still in their minds for each other.

Time was flying by as usual at its own pace, but they both were at the same stage of feelings for each other. However they talked less frequently on the phone, but were regularly on contact through Gmail. Both had feelings for each other but never expressed them. One of the major reasons was their family upbringing. They had conservative families where such things were a complete taboo. They knew if they moved further in their relationship, it was only going to hurt them and also their friendship would get ruined, which they could never afford to lose. They were happy with whatever they were getting in their relationship without any hassles.

They were cherishing each moment they spent with each other. They never discussed their feelings also as they knew it would only spoil their present happiness. They just wanted their friendship to be like this always as they both realised the importance of good friends. Their understanding, their comfort level, their concern for each other were much above anything else for them. As love is more prime to two lovers, it was their friendship for them. They truly were indeed best of friends, but love was also lingering somewhere between them which in their case had converted into a deep friendship... their form of love for each other. They cared about each other at a very holistic level which was not definable by anybody. Their relation was different but really very pure and such a relationship is very difficult to find.

God always gives us somebody to bank upon almost from childhood till our last innings of life. It is the mother from the start who lays our foundation and makes us stand on our feet. Then come friends who share our memories until we marry and get the most dependable person, that is the life partner who always stands by our side as a hard rock.

For Vivan and Anubhuti, it was their friendship which they banked upon forever. They shared their joys but never hesitated to help each other in difficulties better than their other close relations. Such was their unusual loving friendship which remained for a lifetime.

One fine day, Vivan decided to pay a surprise visit to Anubhuti's place. He had a meeting with a client in her city. It was a golden opportunity for him to have a chance to see her. So he was quite excited. He took an early morning flight. After reaching the airport, he took an auto to her place as his meeting was to take place in the afternoon. He was fully aware of her address as once she had disclosed it to him during their talks. So he reached her place easily and rang the bell. Anubhuti was still in her morning dreams. She woke up inquisitively at the sound of the bell and started grooming herself while reaching the door hurriedly. She opened the wooden door and was awestruck at what she saw through the grill. Vivan smiled at her shocked expression. She also composed herself and smilingly opened the grill door for him. Anubhuti asked Vivan, "Hey... how come you are here and also without even bothering to inform me."

Vivan was listening to her dumbstruck. She was smiling at him and he just realised to his utter surprise, "Oh... ya... am I here?"

Anubhuti laughed aloud and so did Vivan. After a while, she inquired of him, "Would you like to get freshened up?"

He nodded and she showed him the way to the washroom. Meanwhile, Anubhuti started preparing coffee doing the requisite preparations. She was facing towards the kitchen window enjoying the morning view while making the coffee latte. Suddenly, she felt Vivan's presence. She turned to check and he was there admiring her. Vivan became self-conscious and started looking here and there. Anubhuti also let him ignore her and smiled viciously. She poured hot milk into the coffee mug and asked him, "How much sugar?"

Vivan said, "Two tablespoons."

She put sugar accordingly and handed him his coffee. He shows gratitude saying, "Thank you."

She just smiled at him. He didn't ask her about her coffee as he knew she would take anything only after her bath and prayers. He had discovered this habit of hers on the very first day they met as she didn't have anything in the morning because of her morning ritual.

Vivan teases her, "Tumhara pati bahut khush rahega... nice coffee... haan."

She smilingly confirmed, "Haan woh toh hai."

Anubhuti then asked Vivan, "What are your plans for today then?"

He replied after much thought, "Nothing much... just a meeting with the client at 3. It will hardly take half an hour. What about you?"

She hastily said, "Hmm... good... I have work, but if you wish, I can compensate a leave for you. What do you say?"

Vivan's happiness could be felt in his tone as he said, "Ya... you should... because I will be leaving tomorrow morning."

Anubhuti hid her sadness remarking, "Oh ya... ok then... let's enjoy today."

She left towards the washroom to get ready.

Vivan was examining the house with every sip of his coffee, noting how well she had organised everything all by herself. He was lost in his thoughts when suddenly he saw her. She was looking like a complete diva with hair falling on her rosy glowing face as she was drying it with her towel. Vivan was watching her dumbstruck until Anubhuti caught sight of him. He changed his expression quickly realising that her eyes were on him and gave her a small smile. She too advanced him the same and departed to her room. Vivan heaved a sigh of relief as if he had saved himself from committing a serious crime and got into the washroom to get ready.

Anubhuti finished her puja after getting ready. She wore a beaded bright pink kurti with white leggings. Along with them, she puts on silver coloured crystal hanging earrings and silver flats. No doubt she was looking amazing with her hair open. Vivan too got ready in a white shirt and black trousers looking quite handsome. Both decided to have brunch outside. They took an auto and decided to go to a famous place "Hyderabad House" known for its delicious biryanis. On their way, both indulged in watching the outside scenario. Vivan casually turned to Anubhuti. He just couldn't keep his eyes off her as her hair was playing on her face with the flow of wind. She looked extremely charming. Vivan was staring at her for a while until Anubhuti caught his sight. Vivan quickly turned uncomfortably in the opposite direction. Anubhuti smiled and looked outside again. They reached their destination within an hour. Anubhuti tried to pay for the auto fare but Vivan restrained her.

They proceeded to the entrance of the restaurant. Vivan came forward to open the gate for her. Anubhuti smiled shyly and signalled "thanks" to him which he reciprocated with a grand gesture by putting his hand on his heart. Both of them entered and looked around. The restro was medium-occupied. The Manager of the restro comes towards them delegating them to a two-seated corner table. Vivan offers her a chair. Anubhuti smilingly sat down. Vivan also settled himself. The waiter arrived and asked for the order. Vivan glanced at Anubhuti. She said, "Today your choice."

Vivan replied, "Ok... sure madame."

He ordered Manchurian and noodles with two cold drinks. The waiter left after noting down the order carefully.

Vivan offered Anubhuti a glass of water placed by the waiter beforehand. She accepted it courteously. Vivan took sips of water from his glass. Anubhuti teased him saying, "Tum kab se Chinese khane lage?"

He smiled and replied, "Jab se aap mile ho."

Anubhuti smirked at him and both laughed. The restaurant offered very quick service as soon the waiter arrived with the food. They composed themselves. The waiter placed the food in front of them very professionally, and left. Vivan asked, "May I?" before Anubhuti could think what to say. She smiled and said, "Yes, please."

Vivan placed some food on two plates and offered one to Anubhuti. She was looking at him continuously before she realised that Vivan was noticing her. She became self-conscious and took her plate from him. Vivan hid his naughty smile so that Anubhuti doesn't feel embarrassed, and started eating. She too busied herself with eating, and that moment passed. After some time, Vivan asked, "How is the food?" She replied, "Good."

He jokingly asked, "Just good? But you knew already that the food is good, because you have eaten here earlier as well, right?"

Both laughed, enjoying the joke, and knowing each other's feelings. They called the waiter for the bill. As the waiter brought the bill, Anubhuti hurriedly took it from him. Vivan looked at her questioningly, to which she replied, "Just this one time, I shall pay... It's my right as you are visiting my place..." To this, Vivan replied, "As you order, madame."

Anubhuti quickly put the charged sum on the bill folder and the waiter took it away.

They left the restaurant. It was now 2 pm and time for Vivan to go for his meeting. He asked Anubhuti, "What's the plan now?"

She replied, "I think I would wait for you at home."

He replied, "Fine, then. See you at home,"

Both of them left in their separate directions.

Suddenly the bell rang and Anubhuti quickly rushed towards the main door of her house. It was obviously Vivan holding her favourite roses in his hands. She gave her a welcoming smile to which he also reciprocates in the same manner. Vivan gave her the flowers and she shyly said, "Thanx." Vivan settled himself at the dining table. Anubhuti asked him, "What would you like to have?" after placing the flowers on the table vase. Vivan glanced at her for a while and said, "Coffee with you." She smiled and said, "Ok... sure."

While Anubhuti was engrossed in making coffee, Vivan watched her intently. After finishing, when she handed him the coffee, he quickly directed his attention to the flower vase. Anubhuti knew that he has done this deliberately, so she just ignored the situation so that Vivan did not become self-conscious.

Vivan admired her coffee. She said, "Thanks" while sipping her coffee. She was sitting near his chair so Vivan couldn't resist himself from holding her hand. She became conscious and asked, "What?"

Vivan said nothing and just smiled. She removed her hand from his abruptly. Vivan began to laugh. Anubhuti smirked at him and asked, "What now?" He replies laughingly "Nothing."

Vivan asked Anubhuti, "Would you like to go out again or wanna stay at home?"

She thought for a while and replied "hmm... as you wish. What's your mood?"

He teased her saying, "Mera mood toh bahut kuch hai but I can't."

She looked deeply into his eyes saying, "you na."

He reverted, "What me?" and both just smiled softly looking lovingly at each other.

They both decide to hang out at a nearby mall. They decide to walk there. Vivan could feel her perfume's fragrance while walking so close to her. He was getting mesmerised by her when suddenly Anubhuti's hand struck him accidentally. Both looked so intently at each other before they realised that they had reached the mall. They entered and looked around. They then decided to stroll around. Both were thinking of each other in their minds and were walking in silence.

Vivan said to Anubhuti, "I would like to buy a b'irthday present for you."

She hesitantly said, "No."

He forced her and holding her hand tightly took her to Shoppers Stop. She tried to say "No" but couldn't. They both look around in the shop. Vivan then asks her to try on a pair of jeggings and a top. She couldn't refuse him and didn't want to hurt his feelings, so she went to the trial room. Vivan was astonished to see her when she came out in that dress. She was looking like a princess and was extremely beautiful. She asks him "Is it looking fine on me?"

He said teasing her, "Ok... ok," and laughed. She gave him a soft punch on his hand annoyingly but smilingly. He suddenly hugged her and she became self-conscious. She was happy but looks around shyly. She left him quickly and went to the trial room for changing.

Vivan felt so happy. She returned in a while and saw Vivan smiling. She smiled softly looking at him. Vivan took the chosen dress from her and they went to the billing counter. Vivan took out his credit card. Anubhuti stopped him saying, "No" but he signalled her to be silent. Vivan paid for the dress and the counter girl handed him the dress in a bag. Both of them left the shop. Vivan asks her to have some evening snacks as it was already 7 in the evening.

They decided to go to Costa Coffee outlet in the mall. The waitress asked for the order as they both found a corner table with two seats and sat down comfortably. Vivan asked Anubhuti, "What would you like to have?" She said she would love to have vanilla cappuccino. Vivan ordered one hazelnut and one vanilla cappuccino with his favourite cookies. He paid the bill and the waitress told him that the order would be served at the table itself.

He came back to sit opposite to Anubhuti. She was checking her phone messages. Vivan suddenly held her other hand. She was shocked. Both of them just glanced at each other until the waitress arrived with the order. She dutifully placed the coffees and also served the cookies at the centre of the table.

Vivan asked Anubhuti to have the cookie and the coffee. Both enjoyed their coffee. After a short while, Vivan asked Anubhuti what her plans for the future were. She thought for a while and replied seriously, "Hmm… I have a passion for writing… I would like to pursue writing as a professional in future after quitting the job." Vivan gave her his cutest smile. She too reciprocated in the same manner. Both finished their coffees and cookies. Vivan held the gate open for her. She shyly exited.

After that they went to see a musical event organised in the mall by FMcity. They too stood in the crowd to watch the singer's live performance. It was the famous singer Surjit's live concert, Anubhuti's favourite singer too. Surjit was crooning his hit number "kyunki tum hi ho" from the movie *Aashiqui 2*. The crowd was getting completely mesmerised by his melodious voice.

Suddenly Anubhuti felt Vivan's hand in hers. She glanced at him lovingly as he was busy enjoying the song. The lyrics of the song were making the scenario more romantic now. As the song ended, Vivan caught Anubhuti watching him. She hesitantly took her hand aside. Vivan asks her where she would like to dine out to reduce her awkwardness. She tries to act normal and replied subtly, "Wherever you like."

They decided to head towards the prominent "Foodilicious" restaurant in the mall. They decided to have "chaat" as both loved spicy food. Anubhuti said to Vivan, "Now let me be the host for you please." Vivan nodded smilingly. They decided to have one plate panipuri and a raj kachori. Anubhuti went to the ordering counter and ordered after paying the requisite amount. She took the receipt and turned to go back. Vivan was waiting for her. Both gave the order receipt to the preparing counter. Meanwhile when they were waiting for their food to be prepared at the counter, Vivan looked at Anubhuti lovingly. She was looking a little upset.

He kept both his hands on her shoulders from behind to revive her mood. She smiled. He came forward and caressed her cheeks with his hands. Vivan asked Anubhuti whether she is fine or not. She assures him saying, "I am fine."

The order arrived. Vivan held the tray and they went upstairs to find seats as floor below was fully crowded. They found a place and sat adjacent to each other. Vivan placed a gol-gappa in Anubhuti's mouth. She too did the same to him. Both enjoyed raj kachori too. Anubhuti asked Vivan, "What else would you like to have?"

Vivan says smilingly, "I think we should have tea now." Anubhuti nodded smilingly.

She lovingly says to Vivan, "I will go and get the tea." Vivan tried to convince her to go along with him, but she declined. Finally, she left. She ordered two elaichi teas. When she went upstairs, Vivan said "Hey… Sorry… I should have gone with you."

Anubhuti calmed him down replying, "It's OK dear."

She asked him, "How is the tea?" He happily said, "Good."

He actually liked adrak tea or masala tea, but he went along with Anubhuti's choice, such was his love for her. Anubhuti could feel his love but became hesitant.

Vivan suddenly said, "Hey… I love you a lot."

Anubhuti was shocked by this official revelation. She just couldn't even utter a single word. They both just glanced at each other for a while until they realised it was getting late in the night. Vivan tried to change the scenario by asking Anubhuti, "Hey… Should we go home now?" She quickly replied, " Fine… Sure."

Both stood up and exited.

They looked in opposite directions while walking back home. Suddenly Vivan held her hand. Anubhuti looked at him shocked but happy too. They both realised that they had reached home.

Anubhuti abruptly left Vivan's hand and quickly unlocked the main door of her house. They both entered simultaneously. Anubhuti wished Vivan "goodnight." He hurriedly lifted her hand as she turned to go to her room. She asked anxiously "What?" He glanced at her for a while and then said, "You didn't reply to me."

Anubhuti became silent for a short while and just looked into his eyes.

Vivan too was looking intently into her eyes. Anubhuti hugged Vivan suddenly. He stood dumbstruck, yet was thrilled. He also put his hands around her and hugged her tightly. They were enjoying the precious moment until Anubhuti realised what she was doing. She felt awkward, so she withdrew from Vivan quickly and went into her room.

Vivan had an early morning flight, so he just slept on the drawing room couch thinking about Anubhuti. Vivan heard Anubhuti saying to him, "utho… Jaldi… Nhi toh flight miss ho jayegi."

He woke up hurriedly. Anubhuti laughed at him loudly.

He quickly freshened up and packed his stuff. Only two hours remained for the flight to take off. Vivan and Anubhuti left for the airport taking a cab which Anubhuti had already booked for them. Vivan thanked her. She smiled looking lovingly at him. They reached the airport on time.

Before leaving her, Vivan became emotional and hugged her tightly. Anubhuti too had tears in her eyes. Vivan wiped her eyes saying, "We will be in touch always."

Anubhuti nodded approvingly. Vivan left with his luggage. Anubhuti watched him until he vanished out of her sight. She then left for her home.

Many days passed by as usual. Both of them contacted through Gmail or sometimes called each other. Both were missing each other but never expressed their feelings openly. They knew things would only complicate and they didn't want to ruin their precious friendship which was more important for them than love. "Because good friends are very rare in this world." This was their outlook which helped them also in future to keep their relationship intact.

PART-4

"Unique bond formed of understanding, commitment and maturity not bounded by external factors."

– By thoughtful girl

Decision Time: When Real Decision Changes Their Lives Forever

Vivan and Anubhuti no doubt were truly and madly in love with each other, but there was something which was preventing both of them from confessing their true feelings to each other.

It was Diwali holidays for Anubhuti. She had come home. Vivan too was at his home for the Diwali leave. Both were aware of this as they had already talked through Gmail before coming home. Both had only a week's leave.

So, one fine day they both decided to meet at their favourite place "CCD" at Kamla Nagar. This meeting changed their lives forever.

As usual Vivan was waiting for her. Anubhuti reached there at the decided time, and found Vivan waiting for her at their previous favourite seat. She went up to him and said, "Hi." Vivan replied "hey" amicably. Anubhuti sat adjacent to him. The waiter arrived to serve the order. Vivan had ordered two cappuccinos. The waiter left after placing two glasses full of water.

Vivan asked Anubhuti how she was. She replied politely, "I am good. What about you?"

He smilingly said, "I am fine too." Both glanced at each other for a while. Vivan signalled the waiter. The waiter arrived with two cappuccinos for which Vivan had already paid in advance before Anubhuti's arrival. He had asked him to serve when asked. Also, he had asked him to serve water when Anubhuti arrives on personal request.

Vivan and Anubhuti both sipped their coffees. Suddenly, Vivan asks Anubhuti, "What is your answer? Have you decided something or not?"

She remained silent for a short while. Vivan held her hand lovingly. She looked into his eyes with deep affection.

Abruptly, she slid her hand aside. Vivan looks at her quizzically. She looked away from him. Vivan held her face and tilted it to his side. There were tears in her eyes.

Vivan couldn't bear to see even a single tear in her eyes. So he scolded her and wiped away her tears affectionately.

Anubhuti tried to give a fake smile, but Vivan could feel her sadness from within her heart. Such a great bond had developed between them. Vivan knew himself too how difficult things were, but he always wanted Anubhuti to be happy in her life. The same was true with Anubhuti too. They both respected their relationship as well as themselves.

Suddenly, Anubhuti said to Vivan, "I am just coming." She went towards the washroom. Quickly Anubhuti gave a paper note to the waiter and signalled him towards Vivan. She left hurriedly so that Vivan could not notice her.

The waiter went up to Vivan and gave him the note. Vivan asked him who had given it. The waiter replied with a smile, "The girl who was sitting with you."

Vivan reads in shock the note. "Hey Vivan... I am really sorry... I couldn't face you... So left... We had a great time together... Those memories will always be with me... But our relation can't be more than friends... We are great friends and will always be... Hoping for a great life ahead for you forever... With love and respect... Your friend Anubhuti."

On the way back home, Vivan remembered every moment with Anubhuti. On the other hand, Anubhuti too was very upset. She didn't speak to anybody at home. The day ended on a sad note for them both. Their friendship was still there but love had to be suppressed. Both decided in their minds to keep each other in their hearts forever, the only way to cherish their relationship always.

Vivan and Anubhuti were way beyond their age in terms of understanding, commitment and maturity levels of a relationship. Their bond was at a different level which was not bounded by any external factors.

But indeed, their fate was playing games in all ways. It was creating situations which were not in their hands. This went on until another incident.

PART-5

"Some relationships are different."

– By thoughtful girl

New Beginning: A New Era of Relationship Starts

Life was going on a routine basis for both Vivan and Anubhuti until their ways crossed again after two years.

Vivan was in a mall in Delhi. He was shopping for the new flat which he had presented to his parents as their twenty-fifth marriage anniversary gift. Suddenly, he was interrupted by a girl, "Hey do you know where electrical appliances are kept in this mall for sale?"

Vivan could not even utter a single word. He stood dumbstruck watching the face of that girl. Not to be surprised, the same was the girl's reaction. Yeah!! We are right!! Vivan meets Anubhuti again!!

Both gathered their reactions back to a normal state and greeted each other. Vivan asked Anubhuti for a coffee. She could not resist his request.

Both went to CCD, their old meeting point. Luckily, Vivan and Anubhuti found their old favourite seating place. Vivan pulled the chair forward for Anubhuti and made himself comfortable too. Their exquisite happiness was evident from their faces well.

Vivan asked Anubhuti whether she would like to have water first. To which she replied smilingly, "No thanks."

He then went up to the ordering counter and placed the order for their old-time favourite coffees. Anubhuti passed him a small smile when he came back. He too reciprocated lovingly.

Both became quiet for a while. Old memories were replaying in their minds. The waiter's arrival with the coffees interrupted their thoughts and brought them back to the present moment.

Both sipped coffee happily. Vivan asked Anubhuti what she was up to nowadays. Anubhuti put the coffee mug on the table and took a deep breath. She said something which shocked Vivan.

Anubhuti spoke after a short silence, "I am married now."

Vivan watched her face with huge disappointment. She could sense his feelings very closely, because first love as it is said is really unforgettable. They both had experienced that feeling once which was to be laid to rest in history now.

"No one has been able to understand why fate plays such games on humans when two people meet, fall in love and have to eventually leave each other."

Vivan composed himself and playfully asked Anubhuti, "How is your hubby?"

She glanced at him and then replied with utmost courage, "Very nice."

Both started sipping their coffees again as it is sometimes best to be silent in certain situations!!

Anubhuti wanted to leave now as soon as possible. She was unable to face Vivan now. So, she made an excuse, "Hey, I have to go now as some important work is pending."

Vivan replied in a disheartened tone, "Ok! As you wish."

Both of them left after bidding "goodbyes" and "see you soon" to each other.

Days went by as usual for both. Both got engrossed in their lives, but some feelings can never be forgotten.

"Some relationships are different…"

Vivan knew very well in his mind that now everything was changed completely whether fortunately or unfortunately in his relationship with Anubhuti. He however was in a difficult phase of his life because hopes were now no more and also moving on was also not so easy because his heart was always captured by only that one person whom he had been waiting for always.

Anubhuti too had to accept her fate as a girl of Indian society, with so-called family norms for a girl. She was carrying out her responsibilities as well as a housewife. Such is life!!

Vivan too got married after much family pressure. Both were living their lives happily because sometimes you are happy to see your loved ones happy.

"But life has more in store for them!!"

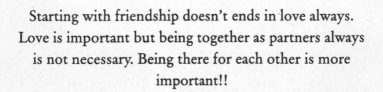

Starting with friendship doesn't ends in love always. Love is important but being together as partners always is not necessary. Being there for each other is more important!!

– By thoughtful girl